Sabrina The Teenage Witch™

Salem's Tails™

CAT TV

Written and Illustrated by

MARK DUBOWSKI

A MINSTREL® BOOK

Published by POCKET BOOKS
New York   London   Toronto   Sydney   Tokyo   Singapore

A MINSTREL PAPERBACK *Original*

 A Minstrel Book published by
POCKET BOOKS, a division of Simon & Schuster Inc.
1230 Avenue of the Americas, New York, NY 10020

Sabrina, The Teenage Witch: Salem's Tails
Based on characters appearing in Archie Comics

And the television series created by Neil Scovell
Developed for television by Jonathan Schmock

Salem quotes taken from the pilot episode
Teleplay by Neil Scovell
Television story by Barney Cohen & Kathryn Wallack

ISBN: 0-671-02102-8

First Minstrel Books printing August 1998

10 9 8 7 6 5 4 3 2 1

A MINSTREL BOOK and colophon are registered trademarks of Simon & Schuster Inc.

SABRINA THE TEENAGE WITCH and all related titles, logos and characters are trademarks of Archie Comics Publications, Inc.

Cover photo by Pat Hill Studio

Printed in the U.S.A.

Dedicated to the adoption center
at the 92nd St. animal shelter,
from a former volunteer

I can't go dancing. I can't make air quotes. The sound of the can opener is the only thing that makes me feel truly alive.

—*Salem*

Chapter 1

"Salem! Come quick!" Sabrina called. She was in the living room, watching TV. "Hurry!"

Salem was in the kitchen, taking a nap.

I can't get up now, Salem dreamed. *I'm a cat, and I'm taking a nap. Taking naps is my job—*

"Hurry, Salem!" Sabrina called again.

Salem raised one eyelid, then let it droop shut. Zzzzzzzzz . . .

Sabrina frowned and waggled her finger. A little puff of light blew across the

1

living room, wafted down the hall, and twinkled into the kitchen.

The magic light swooped under Salem's blanket and lifted him above the kitchen counter.

Whoosh! The blanket sailed toward the living room like a magic carpet. Salem frowned.

It's not easy living with a teenage witch, he thought.

Salem's blanket made a perfect landing in front of the living room TV. On the screen was a huge close-up of another cat's face.

It was a Pretty Kitty Cat Food commercial. The TV cat was named Tobias. He was in all the Pretty Kitty commercials.

A man's voice said, "Pretty Kitty Cat Food is . . ."

"MEOW!" said Tobias.

To show what MEOW meant, white letters flashed across the bottom of the screen: YUMMY!

Sabrina Spellman clicked off the TV and gave Salem a pat on the head. "I knew you wouldn't want to miss Tobias," she said.

"Phooey," Salem complained. "To be perfectly honest, Sabrina, I've seen better acting on a *National Geographic* special."

Sabrina didn't get it. "The animals on *National Geographic* aren't acting," she said.

"That's what I mean," Salem said. "Neither is Tobias!"

"Oh, I get it," Sabrina said. "You're jealous, aren't you?"

Salem's mouth dropped open. "I am *not* jealous!"

"Right." Sabrina smiled.

Salem frowned. "I merely pointed out that Tobias the TV cat's acting skills are, shall we say, underdeveloped."

Sabrina's face made a pained expression.

"Well, think about it!" Salem argued. "He has one line to say in the whole commercial."

"You mean 'Meowww'?"

"Exactly," Salem said, wagging his head. "And he blows it! He does it so badly, they have to use subtitles!"

"You mean where they put the word YUMMY on the screen?" Now she *knew* Salem was jealous. "That's not because he blew it, Salem. That's because he's a *regular* cat! He can't talk like you."

Salem had started out in life as a warlock—a boy with the same powers as a witch. But something had happened after he'd grown up. He'd gotten greedy. He'd tried to take over the world.

That was against the rules.

The Witches' Council had to punish him. They gave him a light sentence—he only had to be a cat for a hundred years.

Instead of taking over the world, he'd be taking naps.

"The fact that I can talk and he can't has nothing to do with it," Salem said. "But if you're suggesting that I could do that commercial ten times better than Tobias, I guess I'll have to agree with you."

"Well, that's not exactly what I meant," Sabrina said. "But now that you mention it, maybe you should try out for a commercial. Tobias makes a lot of money, you know."

Salem's ears perked up at that.

Money?

"How much?" he asked.

"I don't know exactly," Sabrina said. "But he's probably the only cat in town with his own limo."

"Limo?" Salem gasped.

"Car, driver, the works. I just read it in the newspaper," Sabrina said.

She found the article in the newspaper recycling box under the sink. A big photo showed the TV cat stepping out of a long white car.

Salem studied the page. "Look!" he said. "According to this, the company that makes the Pretty Kitty Cat Food commercials is right here in Westbridge!"

The article gave the address for an advertising company called Burke & Lewis. One could write to them for a "paw-to-graphed" picture of Tobias.

"Sabrina, there's someone knocking at the door, and I do believe his name is Mr. Golden Opportunity!" Salem crowed.

"Excuse me?" Sabrina asked.

"Don't you see? This is our big chance!" Salem said. "Call Burke and Lewis and tell them there's a new cat in town!"

"You're not really serious, are you?" Sabrina questioned.

"I'll let you ride in my limo," Salem promised.

She cocked an eyebrow at him.

"Pleeeeeeeease?" he begged.

Sabrina put her hands on her hips and looked at the ceiling. Doing a commercial was probably hard work. That didn't sound like Salem.

"I'll donate half my income to the animal shelter!" Salem pledged.

"Well, that's a switch!" Sabrina said. If Salem would donate to a good cause, how could she say no? "Okay, we'll call them," she said. "The man they interviewed in the newspaper—what was his name?"

"Here it is," Salem said. "Mr. Marvin Denver."

Sabrina looked up the advertising company in the phone book and dialed the number. Salem leaned next to the telephone so he could listen in.

"Burke and Lewis," a lady answered. But before Sabrina could speak, Salem grabbed the phone with his paw.

"Hello," he said. "I have a call from Sabrina Spellman. Returning Marvin Denver's call. It's urgent!"

Sabrina gave Salem the elbow. "He didn't call me!" she whispered.

Salem covered the phone with his paw. "You have to get around the secretaries if you want to talk to the big boys, Sabrina!"

"Hold on a minute," the lady said. She was trying to be helpful.

The phone was silent for a few seconds. Then a man answered.

"Denver."

"It worked!" Salem handed the phone over to Sabrina. "Now butter him up."

"Hello, Mr. Denver?" Sabrina said. "This is Sabrina Spellman. Congratulations on the big article in the newspaper!"

"Who is this?" he asked.

"Sabrina Spellman, Mr. Denver. As I was saying, you must be very proud of the terrific work you're doing there at Burke and Lewis. If you ask me, they ought to call the company DENVER, Burke and Lewis!"

"Well . . ." Clearly, Mr. Denver liked *that* idea.

"I know you're a very busy person. That's why I'm only going to ask for five minutes out of your busy day, Mr. Denver. Just five minutes to introduce you to the next big star in cat TV! His name is Salem, he's a cat, and I'm sure you'll agree, he's quite an actor!"

"Is that right," Mr. Denver said.

Sabrina was on a roll. "I'd be happy to bring him to your office. Would four o'clock tomorrow afternoon be okay, or is four-thirty better?"

You, Sabrina, have a future in tele-marketing, Salem thought.

"What color is your cat?" Mr. Denver asked. Sabrina described Salem's "gleaming" black coat, "bright" eyes, and ability to do "cute" tricks.

"Plus he's very intelligent and obedient. He takes direction *well,*" she emphasized, with a glare at her disobedient cat.

"Four o'clock would be fine," Mr. Denver said, and hung up.

Salem and Sabrina looked at each other and grinned.

"Woo hoo!" they said.

Chapter 2

The next morning, Sabrina's Aunt Zelda came up the front hall stairs with a worried look. "What's wrong with Salem?" she wanted to know.

Sabrina's other aunt, Hilda, came out of her room.

"Meowwww!" came a noise from the first floor of the house.

"What is that weird noise?" Hilda wanted to know.

"It's Salem," Zelda said. "Isn't it strange? He's mewing like a real cat."

"That's not like him," Hilda agreed.

11

Sabrina came out of her room, dressed for school. "I know, I know," she said. "Don't worry, Salem's okay. He's just practicing for a part in a TV commercial."

"TV commercial?" Hilda said. "Cool!"

Zelda was excited, too. "Is he going to be like that other cat? What's his name?"

"Tobias," Sabrina reminded her. "We have a meeting this afternoon with the man who actually makes those commercials. His office is downtown."

"Need a ride there?" Zelda asked. "Hilda and I are going shopping today. We could pick you up after school."

"Meow!" came a howl from downstairs.

"Sounds good to me," Sabrina said, heading downstairs. "Uh—the ride sounds good, that is, not the cat noise. Gotta go!"

After Sabrina went to school and Sabrina's aunts went shopping, Salem was alone. He practiced mewing like a cat for another half-hour before he took a break. He had a snack and read the business section of the newspaper. Then he went into the living room to watch TV.

A Pretty Kitty Cat Food commercial was on. There was Tobias, getting his head petted by a woman's hand.

"Good Tobias," the woman said.

Salem curled his lip and copied her. "Good Tobias!"

Then the woman on TV looked out at Salem and said, "Your cat doesn't have to be a TV star to enjoy the best cat food money can buy!"

Salem frowned.

The picture switched to a bag of Pretty Kitty Cat Food. The woman's voice said, "Because the best cat food money can buy—is Pretty Kitty!"

The picture switched back to a close-up of Tobias. The woman's voice said, "With nine special ingredients to make sure your

cat is as healthy and handsome as Tobias here!"

"Oh, brother!" Salem complained. "As if we don't know he's wearing makeup!"

The woman came back on. She had a coy expression on her face—as if she were sharing a funny secret. "Just don't mention Tobias's limousine—or your cat might want one, too!"

The commercial showed Tobias hopping into the backseat of a long white car. A man in a uniform shut the door for him.

"Well, tee-hee-hee, aren't we clever," Salem groaned.

Then the TV cat stuck his face out the window and the camera zoomed in.

A man's voice said, "Pretty Kitty Cat Food! It's . . ."

"MEOW!" said Tobias.

And the word YUMMY flashed up on the screen.

"The word is *yummy*," Salem said to Tobias's picture on the screen. "Not MEOW! YUMMY, you dummy!"

Salem couldn't wait to show Marvin Denver what he could do.

When Sabrina got home from school, Salem was ready. His coat was brushed and shiny.

"Harvey wished you luck at the tryout," Sabrina said. Harvey was Sabrina's friend at school. He didn't know Salem was really a warlock, but he usually supported anything his pal Sabrina did.

"I won't need luck," Salem said. "Remember, I'm an actor."

"Fine," Sabrina said. "Just remember you're supposed to be a regular cat, too. You can't actually talk. You have to meow, like a cat. Got it?"

"No problemo!" Salem said. "I mean, meow-ow-ow-ow!"

15

Zelda's car beeped in the driveway. Time to go!

They got in the backseat behind Zelda and Hilda. Zelda drove them downtown. They pulled up to a tall office building. Zelda said she and Hilda would be back for them in an hour.

Salem and Sabrina took the elevator to the fourth floor. The doors opened onto a waiting room with sofas and lamps and a TV just like someone's living room. In the back was one long desk where a woman sat and talked on the phone.

Picking up Salem, Sabrina went over to the woman and gave her name.

"Please have a seat," the woman said. Then she punched three or four buttons on the phone and said, "Sabrina Spellman here to see Mr. Denver," then punched some more buttons to get back to the person she was talking to before.

A few minutes later a large man wearing a brightly colored Hawaiian shirt, a white tie, jeans, and cowboy boots appeared in the lobby.

"You Spellman?" he said.

"Sabrina Spellman. How do you do," Sabrina said and put out her hand.

"Call me Denver!" he said in a loud voice. He gave her hand a shake. Then he looked at Salem.

"And this must be Simon!" he said.

"Salem," Sabrina corrected him, before the cat could.

Mr. Denver nodded and waved for them to follow him down the hall. They went to a small room just big enough for a table, chairs, and nothing else and squeezed in.

"OK," said Mr. Denver. "Let's see what Simon the Kitty can do."

"His name is *Salem*," Sabrina reminded him.

1 7

"Gotcha," Mr. Denver said, jabbing his finger in Salem's direction. "You're on!"

"Meowwwwwww!" Salem said. It was a good thing Mr. Denver didn't understand cat language. In cat language, Salem had just told Mr. Denver to get a life.

"Hey, not bad!" Mr. Denver grinned. "Gets your attention and it's slightly annoying—perfect for commercials."

"Mreowwowowowow!" Salem said. Cat language for "And while you're at it, get some clothes. You look like the Ponderosa pineapple picker."

"I like that!" Mr. Denver said. Then he turned to Sabrina. "Tell ya what I'm gonna do!"

First Mr. Denver made Sabrina promise not to repeat anything he told her, since he was about to give her some Top Secret information.

"Pretty Kitty is coming out with a new flavor. The old flavor, Regular, is out."

"What's wrong with Regular?" Sabrina asked him.

Yeah, Salem thought. *That stuff's not bad, for cat food.*

"Nothing," Mr. Denver said. "But the new flavor will cost less to make. A *lot* less."

"Oh, so it will be cheaper to buy in the store," Sabrina said.

"No, it will be more expensive," said Mr. Denver. "A *lot* more expensive."

"I don't understand," said Sabrina. "It costs less to make, but you're going to charge more?"

"It's called advertising, kid," Mr. Denver explained. "We're calling the new stuff New and Improved. That's why we have to charge more. You can't call it New and Improved and charge less, now can you?"

"I guess I see your point, sort of," Sabrina said.

Salem liked the idea. As soon as he got home he was going to call his stockbroker. He needed some shares of Pretty Kitty Cat Food Company stock. When the new product came out, the shares would be worth a lot more money.

The New and Improved cat food was coming out in a fancy black bag. That's why Mr. Denver liked Salem, he explained. Salem was the same color as the new bag.

"I'd like Simon—er, Salem—to be in our next commercial. We'll write up a contract. It will explain what you have to do and how much you get paid."

Salem's eyes got bright when he heard the word *paid*.

Then Mr. Denver got up and shuffled through the narrow place between the chairs and the wall over to the door. "Pick up a bag of the new flavor on your way out," he said. "Someone will call you about the commercial." And then he left.

Salem and Sabrina found their own way out. The lady at the front desk said "congratulations" and gave them a napkin and a small bag. The bag looked like the kind they have on airplanes, in case you got sick. Except it was black, and it was full of cat food. A free sample of Pretty Kitty . . . New and Improved.

Zelda and Hilda were parked in front of the building. They cheered when Sabrina got in the car and told them the news.

"Way to go, Salem!" Zelda said.

"Far out," said Hilda.

"Have some New and Improved cat food, Salem," Sabrina said. She bent back the little wire that held the bag shut and opened it so Salem could have a bite.

Salem ducked his nose into the bag and came up with a nugget of the new food.

21

He rolled it over his tongue to his back teeth and bit down hard. The nugget shattered into tiny pieces. It covered his tongue, filling his mouth with the new taste. Then he swallowed it in one big gulp.

"Well, how is it?" Sabrina asked. Zelda and Hilda looked at him eagerly.

Salem dabbed his mouth with a napkin and cleared his throat.

"It's actually quite . . . gross."

Chapter 3

Quiet on the set!" said a man behind a big TV camera. A bright light above the lens switched on.

"Action!" said Mr. Denver.

Tobias the cat was sitting proudly on a kitchen counter. Behind him, a cardboard wall was painted to look like a kitchen.

They were making a Pretty Kitty commercial.

Salem and Sabrina watched Tobias stare into the camera. He was waiting for a cue—a signal to say his line.

23

Mr. Denver curled his pointer and thumb into an *O*—the sign for OK.

"Meowwwww!" said Tobias.

Salem rolled his eyes.

The camera light stayed on another few seconds. Then Mr. Denver yelled, "CUT!" and the light went out. He looked pleased.

"Good job, Toby," said a woman in a pale green jacket, using Tobias's pet name. She gently scooped him up and took him to a folding chair. The chair had his name across the back. He curled up in the seat and went to sleep.

I can't wait to show that fat cat what real acting is all about, Salem thought.

He and Sabrina walked across the set to say hello to Mr. Denver.

"Ah, yes." Mr. Denver squinted at them. "Miss Spellman and . . ."

"Salem," Sabrina reminded him. "We're really excited to be here, Mr. Denver."

"Hey, this is Hollywood! Big time!" he said. It really wasn't, but it was still exciting.

He studied Salem for a minute. "Better get the star over to makeup. His coat looks a little dull."

I beg your pardon! Salem thought. *There are a few things I could say about your haircut, too, you know.* But the Witches' Council only allowed him to speak to witches and other warlocks, not regular mortals like Mr. Denver.

Sabrina walked Salem over to a table with thin metal legs. On it was a silver brush and comb. No one was around, so Sabrina picked up the brush and worked on Salem's coat.

"Excuse me! Excuse me!" someone cried out. It was the woman in the green jacket. She hurried over to the table.

"Those are *Tobias's* things," she said. She grabbed the brush out of Sabrina's

25

hand and snatched the silver comb off the table.

"Sorry!" Sabrina said. "I really had no idea."

The woman frowned. She looked like she didn't believe it. "Next time, look for the *T*," she said. "All of Tobias's things are engraved with this initial." She held the brush up to the light so Sabrina could see the letter *T* etched on the handle.

"Toby is very particular about his things," she said.

Salem and Sabrina watched her march back to the chair where Tobias was sleeping. Then they saw the star cat looking at them out of one opened eye.

Tobias saw them looking at him and opened the other eye. And he stuck out his tongue.

"Pfttttttttttt!"

Clearly, Tobias didn't like competition. Salem felt like going over and punching

Tobias's lights out. *Get a grip on your-self, Salem,* he thought. *That kind of thinking is what got you in trouble with the Witches' Council in the first place.*

Mr. Denver appeared. "I just filled Salem's bowl with Pretty Kitty New and Improved," he proudly told Sabrina. "But don't let him start on it yet! We need it for the commercial!"

You have nothing to worry about, Salem thought. The thought of eating a bowl of the new cat food gave him a sour stomach. "I don't know if I can go through with this," he told Sabrina after Mr. Denver was gone.

"I don't know what to tell you," Sabrina whispered. "Except maybe it's like certain vegetables—you just have to get used to the taste. You know, like broccoli, squash—"

"I'd rather eat the entire North American winter harvest of broccoli than one

bowl of Pretty Kitty New and Improved," Salem moaned.

Salem and Sabrina waited on the set while Mr. Denver finished a long phone call. The lady in the green jacket was brushing Tobias's coat and cooing at him.

What we need right now is a little magic, Salem thought. He had a great idea.

"What I'm thinking, Sabrina," he whispered, "is how good New and Improved could taste, if we just add a little magic to the recipe. Not a lot. Just enough to get me through the commercial."

Sabrina frowned. "You mean, change the flavor?"

Salem's eyes got big. "Great idea, Sabrina," he said, pretending it was her idea. "Give it a cheesy taste, will you? A hint of tuna and a dash of pepper would be nice, too."

Sabrina shook her head. "That would

be cheating," she told him. "Anyway, I'm sure they have to use the real cat food when they make these commercials."

"Oh, wake up and smell the coffee, Sabrina," Salem grouched. "They do this all the time in dog food work—on TV, it looks like Woofie Chow, but those bowls are really full of chopped T-bone."

"Maybe so," Sabrina said. "But that doesn't make it right. Come to think of it, if you really don't like the new flavor, maybe you shouldn't be doing the commercial."

Salem looked pitiful. "But then how will I get my limo?"

Poor Salem. He really had his heart set on a limousine.

"Miss Spellman, would you mind bringing your cat over to the other set for a lighting check?" said the cameraman.

They were setting up in front of a large white background.

Mr. Denver walked over to explain the idea to Sabrina.

"In this commercial, Salem will actually be inside the new cat food bag. When I give the OK sign, you make him stick his head out. Then make him jump out. He walks to the bowl of cat food and digs in. Then when I point, he looks up and talks."

Something from Shakespeare? Salem thought. *Hamlet? A Midsummer Night's Dream? Or maybe one of the speeches I gave as a warlock. . . .*

"We can handle that." Sabrina nodded.

When everything was ready, Sabrina helped Salem into the black cat food bag and stepped back. "Good luck," she whispered.

"Quiet on the set!" yelled Mr. Denver.

The camera light flared.

Mr. Denver was doing the voice for the commercial. He read loudly from a sheet of paper. "Pretty Kitty Cat Food is letting the cat . . ."

He stopped and gave the OK sign to Sabrina. Sabrina cleared her throat— *Ahem!*—and Salem looked out of the bag. He didn't really need the cue, but he had to *pretend* he was a regular cat. The studio lights were blinding.

"out of the bag!" Mr. Denver finished. Salem bounded out of the bag, onto the floor.

Then Salem walked slowly toward the bowl of cat food.

Mr. Denver continued. "Now there's New and Improved Pretty Kitty Cat Food. More expensive than Regular Flavor, but isn't your cat worth it?"

Salem stared at the bowl of horrible-tasting New and Improved.

Mr. Denver said, "It's really delicious!"

You mean really disgusting, thought Salem.

He stared at the bowl.

The seconds passed like hours.

I've got to have that limo, Salem thought.

Everyone was waiting.

I'll just have to use my imagination, Salem thought. *I'll pretend my airplane crashed in the desert. I've been walking for days. The only thing I've had to eat or drink is a little water sucked from a cactus. Finally I come to a restaurant. A Chinese restaurant. Egg rolls. Fried rice. Chicken with sweet and sour sauce . . .*

He ate hungrily from the bowl.

Out of the corner of his eye he saw something. Mr. Denver was jabbing a finger at him. Talk! Talk!

Salem looked at the camera and went "Mreooooowwwwww!"

"Cut!" Mr. Denver said. "Good rehearsal, Salem!"

Salem gulped. The horrible cat food stuck in his throat. *Did he say REHEARSAL? As in practice? Not the real thing?*

Mr. Denver put down the script—the typed-up version of the commercial. "Take a five-minute break, everybody! Then we'll do it again with some tape in the camera!"

The whole experience left a bitter taste in Salem's mouth.

Or maybe that was just the cat food.

Salem caught a glimpse of Tobias. He was curled up happily in his chair. The lady in the green jacket poured food from a black bag into his bright silver bowl.

How can Tobias eat that stuff?

Salem had no idea.

Chapter 4

"Please, Sabrina. Pleeeeeease . . ." Once they were alone and away from the set, Salem begged Sabrina to cast a spell to change the taste of New and Improved.

"It's like eating leftovers from your school cafeteria—only crunchy," Salem pleaded.

"I'm sorry, Salem," Sabrina said. "I can't use magic every time there's a little problem. That's not the way to solve things."

"Well, thank you very much, Miss

Goody Two-Shoes," Salem grouched. "Can you at least get me something for my tummy? There's a drugstore downstairs."

"That I can do," Sabrina said, and she headed for the elevator.

When she was gone, Salem sat quietly on a folding chair. *Doesn't even have my name on it . . . yet.* He heard the murmur of Mr. Denver talking on the phone. He smelled the ham-on-rye sandwich the cameraman was having for lunch. He saw Tobias asleep in his special chair.

Then he heard a low rustling sound coming from behind a curtain.

Salem strolled over to have a look.

It was the lady in the green jacket. She was pouring cat food from a bag of Regular Pretty Kitty Cat Food. The Regular flavor food was going into a black, New and Improved bag.

So that's it! Salem thought.

Tobias was cheating! He, or his trainer,

probably knew Salem was being groomed as Tobias's replacement. To prove he was loyal, Tobias was eating from the New and Improved bag, but it was really filled with good old Regular Flavor. The lady in the green jacket was switching it for him!

I have to hand it to Tobias. He really knows how to play the game. If you don't like the score, change the rules! Salem thought. *Well, this is one game that TWO can play!*

While everyone was busy off the set, Salem quietly pushed his bowl—the one with New and Improved—over to where Tobias was sleeping.

Then he pushed Tobias's bowl—with yummy Regular Flavor—over to where they were making Salem's commercial.

Now when they shot the commercial, Salem would be eating from Tobias's bowl. It would look just like he was eating New and Improved. But he would really be eating Regular.

No one would know the difference except Salem.

Sometimes my intelligence amazes me, he thought.

A few minutes later, Sabrina was back with something for Salem's stomach. Salem took a tablet and they headed back to the set. "OK, let's all get back to work!" Mr. Denver shouted.

"Pretty Kitty New and Improved Cat Food commercial, take one!"

Sabrina helped Salem into the cat food bag for the shoot.

"Quiet on the set!" Mr. Denver yelled.

But before he could say "action," there was a terrible noise from offstage.

It was Tobias. The lady in the green jacket ran over to see what was the matter.

"It's his bowl," she called out. "He's

got the wrong bowl!" Tobias wasn't happy about it, and neither was the lady.

Salem put on his best It-wasn't-me face.

But the lady in the green jacket had already figured out what had happened. She marched over to the set and held Salem's bowl up to the light. Sure enough, it had the letter T engraved on it.

Mr. Denver shrugged. "That Tobias is really finicky about his bowl," he explained to Sabrina and the cameraman.

The lady in green took Tobias's bowl away from Salem and came back with Salem's yucky New and Improved.

"Pretty Kitty New and Improved, take two," Mr. Denver announced.

They did two more takes after that. Finally Mr. Denver thought they had enough tape. Salem couldn't eat another bowl of New and Improved anyway.

Even if he wanted to. Which he didn't. Ever.

"Don't forget to pick up my paycheck," Salem told Sabrina, burping.

"I already got it," Sabrina said. "But we can't leave yet. Mr. Denver said he needs to talk to us before we go." Sabrina went off in search of Mr. Denver, and Salem plodded behind her.

"There you are," Mr. Denver said when they found each other. "I need your help with another project.

"The Pretty Kitty Cat Food Company wants to do a live taste test at the Westbridge Shopping Center in a week and a half. We'll need you and Salem there, and Tobias of course."

Salem didn't think he could feel any sicker. But he did. *Oh joy,* he thought. *A taste test in front of a LIVE audience.*

"We're going to show people that ten out of ten cats love New and Improved,"

39

Mr. Denver explained. "But to do that, we need nine more cats."

"Wait a minute," Sabrina said. "Salem, plus Tobias, plus nine more cats—that makes eleven."

"Salem doesn't count," Mr. Denver said.

I beg your pardon? Salem thought.

"As soon as this commercial runs," he explained, "everyone will already know that Salem loves New and Improved. We want to show that ten out of ten other cats love it, too, the first time they try it!"

Sabrina looked relieved. "Does that mean Salem won't have to—uh—participate in the tasting?"

"Right. He just has to be there," Mr. Denver said.

Tears of joy sprang to Salem's eyes.

"As long as I can get nine other cats," Mr. Denver said. "Does Salem have any friends we can invite?"

Salem thought about that. Any cat he invited to eat New and Improved would automatically not be his friend.

Sabrina had another idea. "How about the animal shelter?" she said. "They have lots of cats."

Salem could see a light bulb go on over Mr. Denver's head. "Hey! Great idea, kid!" Mr. Denver said. His eyes got bright. "We can even donate some money and cat food to the shelter. That'll get more people to come to the taste test!"

Sabrina had to carry Salem to the car, he was so stuffed with food.

"Rough day, huh, Salem?" Zelda said.

Hilda gave him a pet. "Aw. He looks like a little rag doll kitty."

Salem croaked something. No one understood until Sabrina leaned close and listened.

"He's saying 'paycheck, paycheck . . .' "

Sabrina told them. She pulled the envelope out of her jeans and tore it open.

"Give it to me straight, Sabrina," Salem moaned. "Is it enough to buy the limo?"

"Sorry, Salem," Sabrina answered. "It's a lot, but not enough for a limo. Not yet, anyway. But you'll get more when you work the taste test."

For now Salem was happy enough just going to sleep in the aunts' car.

Sabrina, her aunts, and Harvey all sat down and watched the news. Salem curled up between Sabrina and Harvey, ready to preen and bask in his stardom. They found out about a traffic jam, tomorrow's weather, and the woman who was running for town council. Then the commercials came on.

The very first one was for Pretty Kitty!

"Salem! Look!" Sabrina yelled.

Salem, who was dozing off for his fourteenth nap of the day, looked up just in time to see his face filling the TV screen. He looked huge!

"Pretty Kitty Cat Food is letting the cat out of the bag!" a man's voice boomed. It was not Mr. Denver's. *Clearly somebody replaced him,* Salem thought smugly.

"New and Improved Pretty Kitty Cat Food costs more than other cat foods, but isn't your cat worth it?" the voice continued.

45

Salem watched himself leap out of the bag in slow motion and head for the food bowl. He dug into the New and Improved as if it were his favorite meal in the whole world.

Now that's what I call acting! Salem thought. *No one can tell I'm pretending it's a bucket of tuna!*

"Remember!" the voice said. "New and Improved Pretty Kitty! It's . . ."

"MEOOOOOWWWWIE!" Salem's picture roared.

The word YUMMIER appeared across the bottom of the screen.

Everyone in the room started clapping.

"Yay, Salem!" Sabrina hooted. "Woo hoo!"

Harvey grinned. Hilda and Zelda looked proud.

For once Salem was actually glad he was

a cat. Being covered with fur meant they couldn't see him blush.

The following Friday Sabrina got a call after school from Mr. Denver. He wanted to make sure they were ready for the taste test tomorrow.

Salem leaned his ear close to the phone.

"That animal shelter idea of yours was great, Sabrina," Mr. Denver said. "They've been a big help. They even gave us a list of everyone who's adopted a cat at the shelter. We sent out over eight hundred invitations."

Salem was horrified. The Westbridge Shopping Center was always crowded on Saturday. Now it would be mobbed. He'd have to be really careful where he laid his tail.

"The Pretty Kitty Company is donating half of everything it makes on Saturday

47

to the Westbridge Shelter," Mr. Denver went on.

"What a coincidence!" Sabrina said. "Salem promised to give half his paycheck to the animal shelter, too!"

Salem moaned. He'd forgotten about that.

"Hey, that's cute—your cat 'promised'?" Mr. Denver said. "We'll have to work that into one of our ads." Sabrina had almost forgotten that Mr. Denver didn't know Salem could talk.

"Imagine the suspense we're building for the taste test," Mr. Denver said. "Everyone will want to know what flavor the kitties will choose—the ever-popular Regular, or New and Improved!"

As the official spokescat for New and Improved, Salem already knew. Regular would win.

By a landslide!

It was going to be the most embarrassing day of his life.

But that's not what Mr. Denver thought. He went on to tell Sabrina he was so sure New and Improved would win by a knockout that he already had a huge banner ready. It said:

10 out of 10 cats love New and Improved.

"It's going to be a disaster," Salem groaned, covering his face with a paw.

"I can't wait," Sabrina said into the phone.

On Saturday Salem woke up with the first known case of terminal stage fright.

"I'm too weak to be a star," Salem trembled. "I'm fading . . . fading . . ."

"Nobody dies from stage fright," Sabrina insisted, pouring him some Regular

Flavor Pretty Kitty. "Get up and get brushed."

"Fading . . . weak . . ."

"You have to go, Salem," Sabrina said. "You promised. And what about your limo?"

"Oh, I'll never be able to save up enough for a real limo," Salem groaned.

"Well, maybe not in just one week," Sabrina admitted. "But there's more to life than riding around in a limo, you know."

Salem looked hurt. "I know that," he said. "I think about the other things, too, you know. The Learjet. The penthouse in New York. The private island in Fiji. Do you have any idea how long it's going to take to get all that stuff?"

"Not exactly what I had in mind," Sabrina said. "I was thinking about the animal shelter, Salem."

Salem looked puzzled. "What would

the animal shelter do with a Learjet?" he wondered.

"You really don't get it, do you," Sabrina said. "In addition to your paycheck, the Pretty Kitty Company is donating a lot of money to the animal shelter for all their help today. And remember, the shelter's doing it with *volunteers,* who aren't getting paid, like you."

"Sometimes I can be such a hairball," Salem admitted.

A half-hour later Zelda was letting them off at the shopping center. "Good luck!" she called.

"Thanks, Aunt Zelda," Sabrina said.

"Don't worry, Zelda. Mr. Denver's bringing plenty of luck with him," Salem added.

"What does that mean?" Sabrina wondered as Zelda drove off.

"Ever hear the expression 'shooting fish

in a barrel,' Sabrina?" Salem asked. "I assure you, Mr. Denver won't leave the results of the taste test up to a bunch of stray cats. There's got to be a trick."

"You're kidding!" Sabrina said. "You don't actually think Mr. Denver's going to cheat, do you?"

"No, I don't *think* he's going to cheat— I *know* it."

Chapter 6

It was a beautiful day for a taste test. The sky was blue, the stores were open, and the parking lot was full at the Westbridge Shopping Center.

Dozens of volunteers were there from the animal shelter. They were helping Mr. Denver set up all the tables, chairs, microphones, and litter boxes needed for a successful event.

The main stage was set up with ten runways—side-by-side with a long table covered with white paper.

Behind the runways was a podium with

a microphone. On either side of the stage were tall stacks of enormous speakers. They looked big enough to play the emergency broadcast signal for the entire planet.

Above it all was a huge banner. Right now, the banner was covered. A long cord dropped from one end.

"I hate to think what's under that covered banner," Salem said.

"Silly, you know," Sabrina said. "Mr. Denver told us. It says ten out of ten cats love New and Improved."

"Talk about counting your chickens before they hatch!" Salem said. "What if something goes wrong?"

"I thought you were sure it wouldn't," Sabrina reminded him. "You said there was a trick."

"I didn't say the trick was going to work, Sabrina," Salem said. "Things can go wrong, you know. Look at what happened to Julius Caesar. One minute you've got the whole world on a string . . . the next minute, poof! You're history."

"What do you think the trick is?"

"I have no idea," Salem said. "My sources have all dried up—I haven't heard a word. It must be very hush-hush."

"I just can't believe Mr. Denver would fix the results." Sabrina pouted. "He seems like a nice man—sort of."

"Welcome to the real world of Cat TV," Salem told her. "It's a jungle out there."

Just then a large potted palm tree walked up and plopped down in front of them. A man stepped out from behind it. It was Mr. Denver. He was on his way to the stage with the plant.

"Sabrina! Salem! Nice to see you!" He grinned. "How about giving me a hand with this tree?"

Sabrina helped Mr. Denver lug the tree

up to the stage behind the speaker's podium. Salem tagged along.

While they were on the stage, Mr. Denver offered to show Sabrina how it was going to work.

"Salem can demonstrate," Mr. Denver said. He scooped Salem up onto one of the long paper-covered tables. It was tilted higher in the back. Salem had to dig in with his claws to keep from slipping down to the front of the stage. *Yikes!*

"First we'll bring out the nine Test Kitties from the animal shelter," he explained. "They'll all start at the same time from the high end of the runways.

"At the other end of the runway, near the front of the stage, we'll have two bowls of cat food. One bowl of Regular Flavor, and one bowl of New and Improved. When I give the signal, the volunteers from the shelter will let the cats go."

That's when the trouble will begin, Salem thought.

"That's when the taste test will begin," Mr. Denver went on. "The kitties will scamper down the runway and choose their favorite. Will it be Regular? Or New and Improved?"

Oh, please, Salem thought. *Spare us the dramatics.* Salem was losing confidence in Mr. Denver. The man actually seemed to *believe* what he was saying. Was it possible he was going to run a fair and honest taste test? Was he not going to lie and cheat in the name of Profit and Plunder?

"Burke and Lewis and the Pretty Kitty Cat Food Company are absolutely certain that nine out of nine kitties from the shelter will love New and Improved."

He said it as if he were pledging allegiance to the flag.

Salem felt like kicking himself. He knew he'd forgotten something. He meant

to sell his Pretty Kitty stock before the taste test, just in case something went wrong. Now Salem was sure the whole thing was doomed. Pretty Kitty was going down the tubes!

"We'll save the big surprise for last," Mr. Denver whispered. "Test Kitty Number Ten will be Tobias himself! Everyone knows how much Tobias loves Pretty Kitty Regular. Will he make the switch to New and Improved?"

Do pigs have wings? Salem thought. *Of course he won't switch.*

"Don't tell me, Mr. Denver," Sabrina said. "I want to be surprised along with everybody else."

Chapter 7

Attention!" Mr. Denver said into the tiny microphone.

An ear-splitting noise blasted from the speakers.

WAHNNNNNNNNNNNNNNNNNN! Feedback. A crowd of shoppers stopped and clutched their ears.

"Check—check—check," Mr. Denver said. As he turned a dial on the microphone, his voice dimmed. "Is that better?"

About half the shaken shoppers nodded and stuck around in a daze to see

59

the show. Mr. Denver launched into his sales pitch.

"Folks, does anyone here own a cat?" Mr. Denver wanted to know.

About a hundred people were there from the animal shelter's mailing list. They all raised their hands and cheered loudly.

"Well, if you own a cat, or have been thinking about owning a cat, or know someone who owns a cat, then this"—he held up a bag of Pretty Kitty New and Improved—"is definitely for you!"

Salem held a paw to his nose. "Darn, I think we're downwind of the New and Improved supply tent," he snarled.

Sabrina gave him a worried look. "Shhh! I hope the other cats aren't as picky as you," she said.

"Cross your toes," Salem said. "I'm hoping my instincts are wrong, and Mr.

Denver isn't using real New and Improved in the actual taste test."

The aroma of New and Improved coming from the supply tent gave Salem an idea.

"Wait here, Sabrina," he said. "I'll be right back."

"Where are you going now?" Sabrina whispered. "The show's about to begin."

"I've just got to have a look inside that supply tent," Salem told her. "If Mr. Denver has an ace up his sleeve, it's in there. And if I don't know before the actual event, the suspense may just kill me. Later, Sabrina."

Salem skittered around the back of the crowd and slipped under the tent. It was filled with everything Mr. Denver needed to run a taste test. Cat food. Advertising handouts. Folding chairs. A picnic cooler. Clipboards. A bag of chocolate chip cookies marked "MARVIN'S."

Salem stopped at two towers of shiny silver bowls stacked one on top of the other. The taste test bowls!

The bowls were already filled with dry cat food. They had stickers telling whether they were Regular or New and Improved.

Salem sniffed the tower of Regular bowls. It was Pretty Kitty's old flavor, all right. *Not bad . . . for cat food*, he thought.

Then Salem sniffed the other tower of bowls, marked New and Improved.

What other flavor had Mr. Denver substituted for New and Improved? What delightful taste treat would he be using to lure the Test Kitties away from Regular? *Fish? Cheese? Filet mignon?*

Salem breathed in.

Suddenly he felt as if his nose had been hit head-on by a garbage truck. The smell of all those bowls of Pretty Kitty New and Improved at once made his head spin.

Drat! Mr. Denver was running a fair contest! He was using real New and Improved in the taste test. He wasn't going to cheat after all.

Mr. Denver must be out of his mind, Salem thought. No cat worth his whiskers is going to eat that stuff by choice.

Then Salem noticed a curious difference in one bowl—the one with the *T* engraved on the side.

Even though Tobias's bowl had a New and Improved label on the side, there was something fishy about the food. Salem had a nibble.

Just as I suspected, he thought. *The lady in the green jacket must have been here. She must've known Tobias* wouldn't *eat the new food, so she put the old flavor in his New and Improved bowl!*

63

What a cheater! Salem thought. It was sickening. Here was Mr. Denver, trying to run a taste test fair and square. And there was Tobias and the lady in the green jacket, making a mockery of it all, just to save their jobs.

If this ship is going down, Salem thought, *Tobias is going right down with it. And I get to watch!*

Salem took the rim of Tobias's bowl in his mouth, took it to a corner of the tent, and dumped it.

Then he took Tobias's empty bowl to an open bag of New and Improved. He pushed it against the torn top. Then he pawed food into the bowl. Finally he put the bowl back where it belonged on top of the stack labeled New and Improved.

Whew! Being fair is hard work! Salem thought.

But now the taste test was really on the up and up.

Cat TV

Not a moment too soon. Salem was just on his way out when the Taste Test Helpers from the animal shelter came in for the cat food. Salem ducked out the way he had come in.

"My faith in mankind is fully restored," Salem said to Sabrina when he leaped back up into her arms. "Silly humans."

Sabrina knew right away what he meant. "Mr. Denver is using the real cat food for the taste test? He's not going to cheat? The New and Improved bowls are really New and Improved?"

"Except for Tobias's bowl," Salem told her. "Someone gave him the good stuff instead of New and Improved. I'm *sure* it was an accident. I took care of it, though."

"Way to go. That's being a good sport," Sabrina said.

"I just want to be there when that yummy mouthful from Tobias's favorite

bowl turns out to be the toxic taste of New and Improved. The look on Tobias's face will be my reward," Salem purred. "As well as getting *his* spokescat position!"

"Wait a minute," Sabrina worried. "You're sure he won't like New and Improved? And what about the other cats? What if they don't like it, either? Salem— if the taste test doesn't work, the Pretty Kitty Company won't make a donation to the animal shelter. And they might not launch the new flavor. Then they won't need a *new* spokescat!"

Salem frowned. "You're right, Sabrina, although I am glad you finally see the value of trickery and deception. Unfortunately, it's too late to go back and cheat now.

"Here come the kitties."

Chapter 8

Music blasted from the speakers. People cheered. Nine Test Kitty Helpers came out dressed all in black holding nine cats high above their heads.

"It looks like a Broadway musical," Sabrina said. "You know, like that show *Cats*."

Mr. Denver swaggered out with his microphone.

"It looks more like the play *Death of a Salesman* to me," Salem said.

Mr. Denver's voice boomed over the clapping and cheering. "BRING OUT THE

CATS, AND BRING OUT THE FOOD!" he announced. "PRETTY KITTY CAT FOOD ANNOUNCES THE PRETTY KITTY CAT FOOD TASTE TEST!"

Bet you can't say "Pretty Kitty Cat Food Taste Test" ten times real fast, Salem thought.

Nine Food Bowl Helpers came on stage. Each helper carried two bowls—one bowl marked Regular and one bowl marked New and Improved. They set them carefully at the ends of the runways.

"How many people here said they own a cat?" Mr. Denver's voice again blasted from the speakers.

Hands went up all over. People cheered.

"Well, then I don't have to tell you how finicky a cat can be sometimes!" Mr. Denver told them.

Just because we won't eat radioactive waste, Salem thought, *is no reason to call us finicky.*

Cat TV

"Today, we're going to ask some very finicky cats which cat food they prefer: Regular? Or New and Improved—"

The crowd roared. It reminded Salem of the Colosseum in Rome during the time of Emperor Nero. *Ah, those were the days!*

"Test Kitty Helpers, are you ready!" Mr. Denver cried.

The Test Kitty Helpers lowered the nine cats to the runways.

"On your mark, get set, GO!" Mr. Denver screamed.

The crowd went wild.

Nine test kitties skittered down the slippery sloping runways, headed straight for the taste test bowls. People screamed and cheered as the scared kitties tumbled and crashed into the bowls. Salem put both front paws over his eyes. "I can't look!" he wept.

"Get up, Salem! Get up!" Sabrina in-

sisted. She was shaking him. He was hoping she was waking him from a dream. He wanted to open his eyes and find out the Pretty Kitty Cat Food Taste Test was all a dream.

A bad dream.

But when he opened his eyes, it wasn't a dream. And it wasn't bad, either. When Sabrina lifted him up to see what had happened, Salem's jaw dropped open.

"WOO HOO!" Sabrina hooted loudly. It seemed impossible, but it was true. All nine Test Kitties were eating from the New and Improved bowls! Just like they were supposed to!

"I don't get it!" Salem gasped. "That stuff is like roadkill on rye!"

Sabrina knew. "It's just like that day we saw Tobias on TV," she told him. "Remember? You said he couldn't act because he couldn't say 'yummy.' And I told you he couldn't say yummy because he's a normal cat. Not like you."

Salem shook his head. "So?"

"Well," Sabrina said, "the Test Kitties are *normal* cats, too. And normal cats really do like New and Improved better. Face it, Salem, being a warlock for nine hundred years spoiled your taste buds."

She pointed toward the stage. "How many of those cats can say they're graduates of the French Academy of Cooking?"

That brought back memories for Salem. "The academy still serves my Sauce Salem in the faculty dining hall," he said fondly. "After five hundred years."

But Sabrina shook her head. "Unfortunately, the animal shelter is not out of the woods yet. Nine out of nine cats was good—but the sign says ten out of ten."

And look who's up next for the home team, Salem thought. *Tobias. The only*

7 l

cat in the world who might be even more finicky than me!

The crowd hushed. It was so quiet, Salem could almost hear one of the test kitties licking crumbs off its whiskers.

Tobias stood like a statue, clearly milking the moment for everything it was worth. He peered down the long runway to the bowls of Regular and New and Improved, waiting in the distance.

Then he moved. Step by step, he came down the runway.

It was the most agonizing display of overacting Salem had ever witnessed. *And I've seen all the awards shows!*

"I can't take this, Sabrina," Salem whined. "If the suspense doesn't kill me, Tobias's acting will."

"Mr. Denver is the one who's going to get you," Sabrina said, "if he ever finds out you switched Tobias's food."

"I was only trying to be fair," Salem pleaded.

"Uh-huh." Sabrina nodded. But she really didn't believe him. If Salem had left well enough alone, Tobias would be just seconds away from a nice meal of Pretty Kitty Regular.

Everyone would think it was New and Improved. The taste test would look like a success. The animal shelter would get its donation from the cat food company.

But *no*. Salem *had* to have things his way.

Sometimes Salem was more like a cat than he'd ever admit.

Tobias was headed straight for the worst meal of his life. Salem could just imagine the howl of disgust that was coming when the preening cat found New and Improved in his New and Improved bowl. The look of shock on the faces in the

73

crowd. The anger and disappointment in the eyes of the animal shelter volunteers.

Salem's head hung over Sabrina's arm. "What have I done?" he wailed. "It's all my fault. I'm so ashamed!"

Then he looked up as if nothing had happened. "Hey, I've got an idea!" he said and bounded off.

It was a good thing Tobias was taking his time getting down the runway. For two reasons.

It kept the crowd guessing.

And it gave Salem a chance to squeeze his way to the front.

Salem got where he wanted to be just as Tobias came to his favorite bowl. The bowls with the *T* on the outside—and the New and Improved yuck on the inside.

Salem stood on his hind legs and peered over the edge of the runway.

Look at me, Tobias, Salem thought. *Look at me . . . look at me . . . look at me . . .* He was trying to send a mental message to his fellow actor.

At the last second something caught Tobias's eye. Two dark eyes in a small dark head with pointy black ears were staring at him.

And his food bowl!

Salem concentrated. *It's your big chance, Tobias,* he thought. *Your moment in the sun. Let bygones be bygones, Tobias. Actor to actor, I'm begging you, give this performance everything you've got. Tobias, I want the Best Performance of the Year by a Cat out of you on this one. I know you can do it, baby!*

Tobias looked stunned. Was he getting a mental message? *Am I getting through to him?* Salem wondered.

No, he was probably just thinking that Salem wanted his food bowl again.

Then Salem stuck out his tongue. If

that didn't light a fire under Tobias, nothing would!

Pfttttttttttt!

The pampered star of the Pretty Kitty commercials dived into the six-ounce serving of New and Improved cat food like it was a sixty-pound tuna that another cat was eyeing.

For just a second Salem thought he saw Tobias shudder.

The taste of New and Improved has a way of doing that to you, Salem thought. *I feel your pain, Tobias.*

But then the star kitty came up with a roar.

"MEOWWWWWWWWWW!" he howled.

The crowd went crazy. They all screamed together at the top of their lungs—

"YUMMYYYYYYYYYYYYY!"

Chapter 9

Ah, Sorbet au Salem," Salem purred. "My favorite."

"I got it from a book of sixteenth century French recipes," Sabrina said. "I didn't know frozen desserts went back that far."

"I was always ahead of my time," Salem said. "Or in back of it. Depending on the spell."

"Well, you didn't need a magic spell to help Tobias pull off the Pretty Kitty Taste Test. The animal shelter was really happy

7 7

with the money the company donated for helping them out."

"I know," Salem said. "I don't mind telling you I sweetened the pot with a donation of my own. After the taste test, my Pretty Kitty Company stock went up like a rocket. I felt it was only fair to split the profits with those who made it all possible."

"Mr. Denver also told me someone representing *me* called him to say you had retired from advertising, too," Sabrina said.

"My true calling, Sabrina, is not to make commercials, but to watch them from the comfort of the living room couch," he told her.

Just then Zelda and Hilda walked in.

"Don't eat too much of that," Zelda said in her elegant voice.

"Yeah, it's just an appetizer," Hilda said.

Sabrina explained to her cat. "We really appreciate the way you *encouraged* Tobias to make the taste test a success for the animal shelter. They had a lot of adoptions today. To show you how much we appreciate it, we're taking you out to dinner."

"I'd love to, ladies, but cats aren't allowed in restaurants," Salem sighted.

"They are in Paris," Zelda told him. "We understand you're rather partial to French cooking—"

"Paris? Right now?" Salem gasped.

POOF! A pink cloud burst in the room. When the smoke cleared, Salem was looking at a man in a neatly pressed limo driver's uniform.

"Your car is waiting," Sabrina said to Salem.

Salem's eyes brightened. "A limo ride? All the way to Paris? Only three won-

derful witches could pull something like that off."

Tears filled Salem's eyes. "I love you guys," he said. "Now, let's chow—I'm starving for anything Old and Unimproved!"

Cat Care Tips

#1 Make sure your kitty has plenty of fresh water. Change the water at least once a day.

#2 Just like people, animals have different nutritional needs at different stages in their lives. Ask your vet if it's time to change your cat's diet.

#3 Unlike Salem, not all cats can or should eat "people food." Check with your vet to see what's good and what's bad for your pet.

#4 Take your pet to the vet at least once a year for a check-up.

About the Author

Mark Dubowski lives next door to a cat. She comes when Mark calls her. And she's the only cat in the world who won't run when Mark's dog wants to play chase. She pretends she doesn't care, and the dog gives up. Smart cat.

Mark Dubowski's first writing job was to make up an advertisement for a cookie. When he finished the ad, he got to eat the cookie! He is also a cartoonist, illustrates books for younger readers, and has co-written many books with his wife, Cathy East Dubowski.

He and Cathy live in North Carolina with their two daughters, Lauren and Megan, and their golden retriever, Macdougal.

Sabrina The Teenage Witch™

Salem's Tails™

What's it like to be a powerful warlock, sentenced t
one hundred years in a cat's body for trying to tak
over the world?

Ask Salem.

**Read all about Salem's magical adventures in thi
new series based on the hit ABC-TV show**

#1 CAT TV

By Mark Dubowski

Now available!
Look for a new title every every month

A MINSTREL® BOOK

Published by Pocket Books

2007

Do your younger brothers and sisters want to read books like yours?

Let them know there are books just for them!

THE NANCY DREW NOTEBOOKS®

Look for a brand-new story every other month

Available from Minstrel® Books
Published by Pocket Books   1356-01

BRAND-NEW SERIES!

Meet up with suspense and mystery in

FRANK AND JOE HARDY: THE CLUES BROTHERS™

▼

#1 The Gross Ghost Mystery

Frank and Joe are making friends and meeting monsters!

#2 The Karate Clue

Somebody's kicking up a major mess!

#3 First Day, Worst Day

Everybody's mad at Joe! Is he a tattletale?

#4 Jump Shot Detectives

He shoots! He scores! He steals!

#5 Dinosaur Disaster

It's big, it's bad, it's a Bayport-asaurus! Sort-of.

By Franklin W. Dixon

Look for a brand-new story every other month
at your local bookseller

 A MINSTREL® BOOK

Published by Pocket Books

1398-0-

BILL WALLACE

Award-winning author Bill Wallace brings you fun-filled
stories of animals full of humor and exciting adventures.

- ☐ **BEAUTY**..74188-8/$3.9(
- ☐ **RED DOG**...70141-X/$3.9(
- ☐ **TRAPPED IN DEATH CAVE**.................................. 69014-0/$3.9(
- ☐ **A DOG CALLED KITTY**.......................................77081-0/$3.99
- ☐ **DANGER ON PANTHER PEAK**........................ ....70271-8/$3.5(
- ☐ **SNOT STEW**...69335-2/$3.99
- ☐ **FERRET IN THE BEDROOM,**
- ☐ **LIZARDS IN THE FRIDGE**....................................68099-4/$3.5(
- ☐ **DANGER IN QUICKSAND SWAMP**.......................70898-8/$3.99
- ☐ **CHRISTMAS SPURS**...74505-0/$3.5(
- ☐ **TOTALLY DISGUSTING**...75416-5/$3.5(
- ☐ **BUFFALO GAL** ....79899-5/$3.5(
- ☐ **NEVER SAY QUIT**..88264-3/$3.5(
- ☐ **BIGGEST KLUTZ IN FIFTH GRADE**...........................86970-1/$3.99
- ☐ **BLACKWATER SWAMP**...51156-4/$3.5(
- ☐ **WATCHDOG AND THE COYOTES**.............................89075-1/$3.99
- ☐ **TRUE FRIENDS**...53036-4/$3.99
- ☐ **JOURNEY INTO TERROR (paperback)**.......................51999-9/$3.99
- ☐ **THE FINAL FREEDOM (paperback)**.........................53000-3/$3.99
- ☐ **THE BACKWARD BIRD DOG (paperback)**...................56852-3/$3.99
- ☐ **UPCHUCK AND THE ROTTEN WILLY (hardcover)**.01769-1/$14.0(